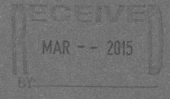

Uncle Eli's WEDDING

TRACY NEWMAN

pictures by
SERNUR ISIK

ALBERT WHITMAN & COMPANY
CHICAGO, ILLINOIS

Daniel tugged at his tie. When would this wedding start? *I should be on the field doing drills with Uncle Eli*, he thought.

But Uncle Eli was inside getting ready.

Daniel spied a soccer ball across the lawn.

He dribbled, kicked the ball, and—wham—slammed it into the bushes.

"Goal!" Daniel whooped, sliding onto his knees.

Bubbe Tillie hurried to Daniel. "Oy! Are you hurt?"

Bubbe Millie scurried to Daniel. "Oy! So much dirt!"

Daniel brushed off his suit. "I was practicing my footwork. Uncle Eli's been too busy with wedding stuff to coach me."

Daniel blasted the ball again. "After Uncle Eli marries Lilah we may never play soccer together. How can we be a team anymore?"

Uncle Eli ran onto the lawn. "It's time! We're starting!"

The rabbi called out to him, "Who's signing your wedding contract?"

"I'll do it," Daniel offered.

Uncle Eli ruffled Daniel's hair. "Sorry, champ. Only adults can sign a *ketubah*. But I promise, before the ceremony ends, we'll find something special to do together."

Daniel followed Uncle Eli into a little room. People surrounded Lilah, fussing over her.

Bubbe Tillie's eyes gleamed. "Look at the *kallah*—a radiant bride!"

Bubbe Millie's face beamed. "Yes, I am *kvelling*—bursting with pride!"

Daniel kicked some rose petals toward Lilah. "I guess you can't watch my footwork now."

"Sorry, buddy," Lilah apologized. "But I know Uncle Eli will find something special to do with you in a little while."

Bubbe Tillie decreed, "*Bubelah*, sit. There's no time to play."

Bubbe Millie agreed, "Aunt Lilah's too busy for footwork today."

"She's not my aunt yet," Daniel grumbled.

The rabbi tapped Uncle Eli's shoulder. "Time to lower the bride's veil."

Bubbe Tillie gushed. "How divine—lace so fine."

Bubbe Millie blushed. "See her shine—that was mine."

Uncle Eli unpinned the filmy veil.

Daniel giggled. "He covered her face!"

Bubbe Tillie hushed. "Shush."

Bubbe Millie shushed. "Hush."

After the guests sat and the music began to play, Lilah waited with Daniel behind a curtain. "Ready to take your turn?" she asked.

Daniel nodded and took off down the long carpeted aisle like he was chasing a soccer ball.

Bubbe Tillie said, "Whoa, *boychik*."

Bubbe Millie pled, "Slow, *boychik*."

Panting, Daniel reached the front of the room. The rabbi and three other men clutched poles.

Bubbe Tillie cooed. "That *chuppah*. Like a beautiful tent!"

Bubbe Millie oohed. "Those flowers. A magnificent scent!"

"Who's going to hold this chuppah pole?" the rabbi asked.

Daniel jumped. "Me!"

"Sorry, champ," Uncle Eli said. "You're not tall enough so I gave that honor to some special grown-ups. But, I promise, soon we'll do something special together."

The rabbi spoke. Daniel wiggled.
Bubbe Tillie cried.

The rabbi sang. Daniel jiggled.
Bubbe Millie sighed.

Finally Uncle Eli stepped forward.

"Is the wedding over?" Daniel asked.

"Eli needs to break the glass—that's my favorite part," said Bubbe Tillie.

"Such a happy moment—it really warms my heart," said Bubbe Millie.

"No fair!" Daniel sniffed. "We didn't do anything special together."

A tear slipped from Daniel's eye as the rabbi placed a napkin folded over a glass on the floor.

Uncle Eli tried to break it and fumbled.

Bubbe Tillie cheered, "Crack it! Shatter it!"

Bubbe Millie volunteered, "Whack it! Batter it!"

What was wrong? Why couldn't Uncle Eli break the glass?

Daniel jumped up to join Uncle Eli and Lilah under the chuppah. "Footwork!" he coached.

Uncle Eli looked at Daniel. Daniel looked at Lilah.
Lilah looked at Uncle Eli.

Lilah nodded. "Here's your chance," she whispered to Daniel. "Something special with Uncle Eli."

Daniel reached for Uncle Eli's hand.
Together they lifted their feet.

And together—smash, crash—
they broke the glass!

Cheery Bubbe Tillie called, "*Mazel Tov!*"

Teary Bubbe Millie bawled, "*Mazel Tov!*"

Daniel took the bride and groom's hands. "Go team!"

Bubbe Tillie waved. "A *simcha*! So sweet."

Bubbe Millie raved, "Such *nachas*! Let's eat!"

A note from the author

Weddings are always joyous occasions, no matter how they are celebrated. I have been fortunate enough to attend Jewish weddings in locations as varied as a beach in Mexico, a synagogue in my hometown, a French chateau, an Italian restaurant, and even my own wedding—in a college alumni clubhouse. All of these diverse venues have been perfectly kosher! Although Jewish weddings may differ widely on where they take place, most include a ketubah, a chuppah, and the always festive, but often stress-inducing, moment when the groom smashes a glass in front of everyone. And afterward, a Jewish wedding celebration ends with lively music, dancing, and delicious food!

Here are a few key words you might hear at a Jewish wedding:

badeken—the veiling of the bride by the groom that takes place before the start of the marriage ceremony

chatan—the Hebrew word for groom

chuppah—the wedding canopy that creates a symbolic private and holy, yet visibly open, space for the bride and groom and which symbolizes the home that the new couple will create

horah—a popular dance that often takes place during a wedding celebration and may continue for an extensive medley of Jewish music

kallah—the Hebrew word for bride

ketubah—the wedding contract that is signed by the bride and groom and witnessed by friends or family before the marriage ceremony

To Mom, Marc, Sharon, and Chris;
and, of course, to my beloved Nanny Rose —TN

Library of Congress Cataloging-in-Publication data is on file with the publisher.

Text copyright © 2015 by Tracy Newman
Pictures copyright © 2015 by Sernur Isik
Published in 2015 by Albert Whitman & Company
ISBN 978-0-8075-8293-0

Printed in China.
10 9 8 7 6 5 4 3 2 1 BP 20 19 18 17 16 15 14

Design by Jordan Kost

For more information about Albert Whitman & Company,
visit our web site at www.albertwhitman.com.